MW00899003

Sabrena Half

FEATURING CROW ARTIST:

Zackery Dean BirdFaraway
Larry Big Lake
Salisha Old Bull

DESIGNED BY:

Kevin Nichols ‖ Ultra Graphics

PUBLISHED BY:

Bakaate, LLC Copyright 2021

# ELK MORNING

## COUNTS HIS FIRST COUP

ARTIST:

Larry Big Lake

Elk Morning was the grandson of Chief Prays in the Morning of the Crow Apsaalooke. To become a great chief like his grandfather, Elk Morning had to show his bravery by doing four courageous deeds known as coups.

The first coup was capturing a very grand horse from one of his rivals.

His grandfather told him to prepare himself, he must first have a Vision Quest. This was a tradition where the Creator would give him instructions on what to do on his quest to count his first coup.

Elk Morning journeyed to the mountains and spent four days and four nights without food and water. His suffering helped him understand why he must go on his adventure. Elk Morning stayed within a circle of rocks by a fire and waited for the Creator to reveal himself.

One day an elk came close to his circle and stayed for hours. One night a wolf came just as close and began to howl. Every night the northern lights revealed a vision of a great horse crossing the sky.

ARTIST:
Salisha Old Bull

2

When he returned, Elk Morning sat with Chief Prays in the Morning and asked him to interpret his vision quest, his rite of passage and how to proceed.

The great chief said, "The elk you saw is your helper. Paint your shield with an elk. The wolf is your disguise. You also saw a horse in the lights in the sky?"

"Yes Grandfather, I saw a great bronze horse with a circle around his eye, four lines on his cheek, a lightning bolt on his leg, a horse track on his shoulder. Finally, there was a hand on its rump as if it were calling me to reach out and touch it."

**"** I know a great bronze horse. He belongs to our rival many miles north and is named Buffalo Wind. He runs as fast as the herd in the middle of a great hunt. He has a golden mane and tail with a bronze muscular frame."

Grandfather continued, "Gather your friends to be your witnesses. They'll testify to your courage."

"What should I tell them Grandfather?"

"Tell them this is the horse that will help you become a great warrior. The circle around his eye is a sign along with the others. Each symbol reveals your future."

Elk Morning looked up to the sky to gather his thoughts.

Grandfather then said, "I know you are afraid Elk Morning, but finding your courage will be your greatest reward."

Elk Morning replied, "I'll be brave and make you proud, Grandfather."

ARTIST:
Salisha Old Bull

Within the week there was a great Crow gathering, with dancing, singing and storytelling. Elk Morning discussed his first coup with his friends Strong Mountain, Brave Hunter, Sacred River, and Carries his Bow. All four of them knew the danger of such a long journey. Anything could happen from falling from your horse to being attacked by a wild animal.

ARTIST:

Zackery Dean BirdFaraway

Strong Mountain said, "My older brother never returned from his first coup attempt. My family suffered two winters from his loss as he was a good hunter."

Still, Elk Morning's friends would go with him and be his witnesses.

He would do the same for them. It was not because of pride but because of the trust they had in their abilities and the love they had for each other.

ARTIST:
Salisha Old Bull

Nearby, Sings Well, Sun Shines Bright, Pretty Braids, and Brings Great Fortune overheard the young men talking. They also knew the danger and had lost brothers in this dangerous rite of passage. They had pride in the men who had returned triumphant as they became great warriors. The young women wanted Elk Morning to be a great chief like his grandfather. First, he had to pass this test.

Elk Morning wanted to talk to the young women before he and his friends left for the rival's camp. He met them the next day as they were helping his mother cure meat from the last buffalo hunt.

Sings Well said, "It's brave of you Elk Morning. You'll come back and your horse will show your bravery."

Sun Shines Bright said, "I prayed for you and your party for a safe journey and safe return home."

Pretty Braids said, "This task is dangerous, many warriors have not come back. Please be alert and safely return home to us."

ARTIST:
Zackery Dean BirdFaraway

ARTIST:
Zackery Dean BirdFaraway

Elk Morning and his friends began their journey to find the great bronze horse. It was many miles north and took several days. They honored Elk Morning's Vision Quest and disguised themselves as wolves.

Far before them in the distance they could see the other tribe's camp covering a large amount of land. They dismounted their own horses and approached quietly.

They hid behind the high rocks so they could take their time and wait until they had a good plan.

ARTIST:

Salisha Old Bull

They spent days watching Buffalo Wind in his pasture surrounded by wild berry bushes. The beautiful animal would treat himself to the pasture grass and bush berries throughout the day.

They watched at night to see Buffalo Wind's owner tie a rope around his neck.

He tied the other end of the rope around his wrist before going to sleep in his tepee.

It would be very difficult for anyone to steal Buffalo Wind with his rope tied to the owner's wrist.

Elk Morning would have to get right next to the owner's tepee, replace the rope with something heavy enough to make the owner think it was Buffalo Wind.

Finally, one night when it was dark enough to stay hidden from the moon, Elk Morning decided to make his move.

Elk Morning sneaked into the camp with his friends watching. He carefully loosened the rope off Buffalo Wind's neck and tied it to a rock, so it still seemed heavy at the end.

The rope moved as if he had awakened the current owner inside the tepee.

Elk Morning froze in place for a moment.

The rope stopped moving and all was quiet again.

Elk Morning carefully stood and stroked Buffalo Wind's neck and opened his hand filled with berries. Buffalo Wind sniffed, smiled, and licked his hand.

The sun was just about to rise as Buffalo Wind followed Elk Morning and the berries away from the tepee without a rope.

At the edge of the enemy camp, Elk Morning grabbed the great horse's mane and jumped on his back.

He hoped he and his friends would get a head start for many miles before the sun was high in the sky.

They ran through rivers and across big rocks and through more rivers to hide their tracks so that the other tribe could not follow them.

The next night, they thought they were being followed. They spent the darkness together without a fire and without sleeping. The moonlight became very bright, and they took turns keeping watch.

Suddenly a sound as large as thunder came from the trees up the hill from where they were hiding. They knew what it was. It was a grizzly bear.

Strong Mountain stood very tall to scare the bear away, but it did not work.

Brave Hunter, Sacred River, and Carries his Bow raised their spears ready to defend themselves from the bear if it charged.

The bear raised up on its hind legs and roared so loud that its voice echoed through the canyon. Its claws were out and shining in the moonlight.

Elk Morning gave the loudest war cry possible. The grizzly dropped down to his front paws and cowered.

The warriors lowered their spears and watched as the bear returned into the dark forest.

ARTIST:

Zackery Dean BirdFaraway

At daybreak, Elk Morning, his horse Buffalo Wind and his friends traveled the remaining miles to the Crow Apsaalooke camp. He had come home proving he had completed his first coup.

Chief Prays in the Morning said, "Capturing the great horse was very brave. Where did you find your courage?"

Elk Morning replied, "I found it in him, grandfather, I knew he was a great horse. He belongs with us because we are a great people."

Then Elk Morning said, "And it's easier to catch a horse with berries than with ropes."

Chief Prays in the Morning said, "Grandson, I know you will soon become a great warrior."

ARTIST:
Salisha Old Bull

A Crow warrior must count four coups to become a chief.

"The most important and the most respected coup was to sneak into an enemy's camp at night and capture a prized horse. The daring warrior had to slip into the camp unnoticed and find such a valued horse in front of the owner's tepee. If the Crow warrior was cunning enough to go into a corral, untie the rope, take the horse out of the camp without waking anybody, and bring it back home, that was an amazing achievement". This coup was called "capturing a horse."

Usually, the horse would be inside a corral or enclosure made of brush poles or logs. Often the horse's neck would be tied with the other end tied of the rope around the wrist of its owner.

Another coup was to touch the first enemy to fall in battle with a hand or even a coup stick.

Another coup was to take away an enemy's weapon such as a knife, tomahawk, spear, or bow.

The last coup was leading a war party.

Joseph Medicine Crow, Counting Coup, Becoming a Crow Chief, National Geographic

ARTIST: Larry Big Lake